CONTENTS

From dawn to dusk, the **SCHOOL BUS OF HORRORS** rumbles along city streets and down country roads, searching for another passenger. Yellow, black markings, dirty windows – it looks like any other school bus.

But **BEWARE!** Step aboard this bus and

experience the scariest ride of your life . . .

CHAPTER ONE
GHOUL BUS

Jordan has one thought on his mind as he stands at the bus stop.

Be cool.

Jordan's friend Evan punches him in the arm.

"Why are you mumbling?"
Evan says.

"What?" says Jordan, rubbing
his arm.

Evan laughs. "You were saying something about a ghoul."

"Ghoul?" Jordan asks.

"Like those one-eyed monsters in the *City of Blood* game," says Evan.

Jordan shakes his head. *Cool, not ghoul,* he thinks.

"You're so weird," says Jordan.

A grin crosses Evan's face.

"Maybe you were saying *girl* and not *ghoul*," says Evan.

"I wasn't," says Jordan.

"I'll bet I know which girl you were mumbling about," says Evan.

A deep rumble shakes the street as a school bus roars to the stop.

"This isn't our bus," says Jordan.

"Maybe the other one broke down," says Evan.

Jordan climbs up into the strange bus. He can't see the bus driver.

He sees only a shadow sitting behind a thick plastic screen.

CHAPTER TWO
A DIFFERENT BUS

It's very dark in here, thinks Jordan.

"What's up, Jordan?" asks a boy
near the door.

Is that really Connor? Jordan asks
himself.

Something looks different.

Then it hits him like a punch in the stomach.

Connor has only one eye in the centre of his forehead!

"Jordan! Over here!" says Evan.

His friend waves him over to a seat.

"Sit with me and Tony," says Evan.

Jordan glances at Tony. He has no ears!

Jordan is frozen with fear.

"It's very quiet in here," says Tony.

Jordan backs away. He stumbles down the aisle.

CHAPTER THREE
A VERY DIFFERENT BUS

With every step, Jordan walks into deeper shadows.

What's going on? he wonders.

The passengers look different from the way they did yesterday.

Jade has a horn growing on the top of her head.

Zac has two tiny red eyes and fins on his neck.

Bryce hisses and sticks out a long, purple tongue.

Don't freak out, Jordan thinks.

As he walks down the dark, gloomy aisle, he finally sees her.

A girl sits at the back of the bus.

It's the girl he's been thinking about all morning.

Be cool, he tells himself. *This is it.*

The girl is sitting alone.

Jordan's stomach feels like a bucket of ice.

He's afraid she might be different like the others.

The girl waves through the
darkness at Jordan.

CHAPTER FOUR
DARK MIRRORS

Jordan sits down next to the girl.

She looks just like she did
yesterday.

I wish she'd smile, thinks Jordan.
She has the most beautiful smile ever.

"Hi, I'm Jordan," he says.

The girl nods.

"I know," she says quietly, hardly moving her lips.

Jordan looks around at the other passengers on the bus.

"I don't know about you," he tells the girl. "But I think something weird is going on."

"Yes," whispers the girl. "I was thinking the same thing."

YYEEEEEEEEE!!

Someone is squealing at the front of the bus.

A second kid squeals. Then another.

The kids are all looking at the windows and pointing.

Jordan looks at the window next to the shy girl.

He can't see out. The window is too dirty.

But that's it, thinks Jordan.

The glassy window is so dark, like a mirror.

They're all seeing what they look like in those mirrors!

The shy girl stands up. She covers her ears.

"Make it stop!" she shouts.

EEEEEEEEEEE! AAAHHHHHHHH!

The squeals and screams continue.

The bus stops.

The door hisses open, and the driver yells, "We're here."

Jordan pulls the girl by the hand.

The two of them follow the flood
of squealing kids getting off the bus.

Jordan quickly looks around.

"We're at school!" he yells.

"Jordan! Are you OK, man?" asks
Evan.

"The squeals," says Jordan.
"All those creatures . . ."

"Squeals? Creatures?" says Evan.

Evan stares at Jordan. "You
really have been playing too much
City of Blood," he says.

Jordan now sees that all the other kids look normal.

The kids from the bus walk into school just like any other day.

Jordan turns to the shy girl.

"Sorry I pulled you off the bus like that," he says.

"That's OK," says the girl.

She gives Jordan a wide smile.

She has no teeth!

"Have a good day at school, kids," calls the driver.

Before the bus door closes, Jordan sees the driver lower his plastic wall. He is staring at them.

Smiling at them.

His mouth is filled with the most beautiful teeth Jordan has ever seen.

GLOSSARY

aisle walkway that runs between the rows of seats on a bus

creature living being, human or animal

ghoul evil being of legend that robs graves and feeds on dead bodies

glance look at something very quickly

grin large, cheerful smile

mumbling speaking quietly and unclearly

passenger someone besides the driver who travels on a bus or other vehicle

squeal high-pitched sound or cry

stumble trip, or walk in an unsteady way

DISCUSS

1. Why do you think this book is called *The Squeals on the Bus*?

2. At the end of the story, why do you think the bus driver's mouth is filled with the most beautiful teeth Jordan has ever seen?

3. What's the scariest bus journey you've ever experienced? What made it so terrifying?

WRITE

1. Create a new title for this book. Then write a paragraph about why you chose your new title.

2. In the story, the bus driver is hidden behind a plastic wall. Draw a picture of how you imagine the bus driver looks, and then write a short story about him or her.

3. Write your own School Bus of Horrors story. Who will the bus pick up next?

MICHAEL DAHL is the author of the Library of Doom series, the Dragonblood books and Michael Dahl's Really Scary Stories. (He wants everyone to know that last title was not his idea.) He was born a few minutes after midnight of April Fool's Day in a thunderstorm, has survived various tornados and hurricanes, as well as an attack from a rampant bunny at night ("It reared up at me!"). He currently lives in a haunted house and once saw a ghost in his high school. He will never travel on a school bus. These stories will explain why.

ILLUSTRATOR

EUAN COOK is an illustrator from London, who enjoys drawing pictures for books and watching foxes and jays out of his window. He also likes walking around looking at broken brickwork, sooty statues and the weird drainpipes and stuff you can find behind old run-down buildings.

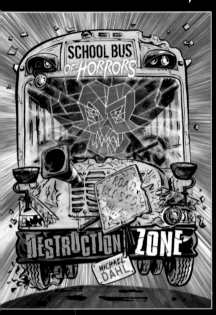